DAYS ARE BEAUTIFUL

100 FLASH FICTION STORIES

ANDREA C. NEIL

Days Are Beautiful, 100 Flash Fiction Stories

Copyright © 2020 by Andrea Neil

All rights reserved.

Paperback ISBN 978-1-7334154-4-6

Published by 1631 Press, LLC

For Durga, who keeps picking up what we keep putting down.

INTRODUCTION

On March 16, 2020, I made the decision to begin sheltering in place, in order to help prevent the spread of COVID-19. By that time, it was apparent that the virus was entrenched in the United States and wasn't going anywhere until it had its way with us. And in March, it was anyone's guess as to how long that would be...

In order to stay home, I gave up my main source of income—teaching public yoga classes. And although I initially started out overjoyed at all the extra time I'd have to work on my next novel, it quickly became apparent that everyone's attention span had gone from short to nonexistent, including my own. I couldn't sleep, I couldn't find a routine, I couldn't settle, no matter how hard I tried. The fear of financial loss was palpable, and fear of the unknown was, on some days, almost unbearable.

Three weeks into my new status of "stay-at-home procrastinating novelist," I came across The 100 Day Project on Instagram. For this annual challenge, participants choose a theme, and post something related to that theme every day for 100 days. The 100 Day Project is great for visual artists, since Instagram is a visual-based platform. And I am, simply put, not a visual artist

— which is why I failed miserably every time I'd tried the project in the past. But on April 7, 2020, the first day of the challenge, at eleven p.m., I decided to take part and write a story every day.

I have written 100-word stories for a long time. I find them easy, yet challenging. Satisfying, yet frustrating. Sometimes flash fiction is vague; sometimes it's incredibly specific. In any case, it's extremely flexible.

Writing 100 words every day seemed achievable and familiar, so I went for it. The first few days were fun. Then I began looking a little closer at the stories, and realized that even though they're fiction, and some seemed to make no sense, they were actually a very detailed and telling account of my experience of staying home during the early days of the Coronavirus Pandemic.

Some characters make multiple appearances and have a story arc that spans the entire book. Some characters are now friends of mine, and I have no doubt will show up in new projects. It has been fun getting to know them all.

As of this writing, we still don't know how things will play out from day to day. And no matter how much I hate to admit it, it seems to me we have all experienced trauma around this event, on many levels. Some may not be felt for a while yet. I personally have never experienced a more divisive, challenging time in my life. Each of us has had to navigate our way through multiple forms of fear, helplessness and supreme frustration. Most days, it still seems surreal.

I try to remind myself to look for what I want to see more of in this world. Some days this is easy. Other days, I fail fantastically. But each day I can wake up and begin again is a beautiful day.

I hope you enjoy these stories, and if you followed along on Instagram as they were released, I hope they brought you some continuity and structure, as they did me. I hope some of them speak to you, or at the very least, make you laugh.

While someday the Coronavirus may fade away into oblivion, the mark it has left on us will not fade for a long time to come. In the meantime, look for what you want to see, tell stories, and most of all, be kind.

Andrea C. Neil

July 2020

April 7, 2020

Day 24

I returned to my study on the second floor, wondering what to do next. I wasn't bored; I was never bored. But I was restless. I sat at my desk to ponder my predicament, but my mind wandered. I gazed out the window, noticing the tree that had begun its springtime growth. Out of the corner of my eye, I caught a glimpse of two small black and white striped birds. Most unusual! Closer inspection revealed they weren't birds, but small cat-like...tigers? And sitting right behind them, on a larger branch, was the mother tiger. Eyeing me hungrily.

April 8, 2020

Crow Convo

I needed a break, so I walked outside and sat in my backyard. Crow flew down from a tree and perched on the fence.

"What's up?" I asked Crow.

"The usual," he answered.

"But the world is a dumpster fire!"

Crow shifted on the fence to look up at the sky. "It is?"

"Well, yeah. I can't even go to the grocery store!"

Crow shrugged. "It does seem quieter."

We looked up at the sky together. I didn't know what to say.

"It's a beautiful day, you know?" It wasn't a question on his part, but a reminder.

April 9, 2020

Golden Days

Oh, kids, let me tell you about the days when we used to go the store and buy things! It was like paradise here on earth. Yes, that's right—we would drive to the store, park, and walk right in! There was bread, eggs, cheese...all the foods you could ever want to eat! There was even toilet paper.

You're not old enough to remember the days when we could go where we wanted and buy what we wanted. And those were the days when we had money for it all, too! Yes, kids, it was a capitalist paradise.

April 10, 2020

Dammit Riker

"Dammit, Riker, I need an answer!"

Sweat breaks out on my forehead. I'm aware the captain is waiting for an answer, but I don't have one for her. How long before we hit the invisible asteroid while traveling faster than light? Would we even hit it at all? Is it even out there?

Modern science and technology should give us all the answers. We're supposedly the smartest beings in the universe. But we constantly forget there are things we cannot see or know. I'd like to think we'll remember one day...but till then, I don't have an answer.

April 11, 2020

Levity Wholesalers

"Levity Wholesalers, thanks for waiting. How can we help?"

"I'd like to order a joke."

"Okay, great. Dirty or clean?"

"Umm, clean, I guess."

"Perfect! Do you know what topic you'd like?"

"Umm…"

"Animal? Political? Hipster? Like that."

"Oh, right. How about animal?"

"Great. Those are back-ordered until next February. Is that okay?"

"Not really; I wanted to get something today."

"All we have for immediate delivery are inappropriate religious jokes. We do have a wide selection of quips on sale, if you're interested?"

"Sure, that'll work."

"Great! I'll connect you with our Quip Department. One moment, please..."

April 12, 2020

Valley Girl

"Oh. My. God. Like, this coffee? It's like, really good?"

Silence.

"Like, it's so totally amazing I'm like, freaking out right now?"

Yes, it's good.

Why can't I have an inner voice that speaks in a regular cadence?

"Oh my god, like, is that a joke? I totally don't know? Tell me!"

Seriously. I don't know how I got stuck with an '80s high-schooler as my inner voice. I bet Einstein didn't have to put up with this crap.

"Andrea, is that, like, a dig? Because, like, you would be sad if I wasn't here."

Like, totally true.

April 13, 2020

War Games

Late Monday afternoon, Durga grew tired of her PlayStation and decided to take a walk. She ran into Shiva, washing his SUV in his driveway.

"Isn't it a little cold to be washing your car?" Durga asked, eyeing the weeds starting to grow between the cement slabs of her neighbor's sidewalk. He'd really been letting the place go lately.

"Perhaps," he answered, setting down the hose. He began drying off his vehicle with the shammy he'd bought one night off TV during a bout of insomnia. "But I need to be ready to roll."

Durga nodded, understanding perfectly.

April 14, 2020

Forward Backward

Diane jammed her foot onto the gas pedal, but nothing happened.

"Dammit, Jim, the thing won't go!" she yelled out the open window of the car.

Jim, who was sitting on the front step reading a book, looked up slowly. "Turn the car on, Diane."

"Oh."

Diane turned the key and the engine roared to life. She jammed her foot on the gas again.

"Jim! It's not going anywhere!"

Jim closed the book, set it down, and put his elbows on his knees. "Put it in gear."

"Oh. Right."

Diane shifted the car into gear and floored it.

April 15, 2020

Doctor JJ

Doctor JJ here, checking in with your daily dose of quarantine posture tips. Now, I know what's on everyone's mind: how can I get that maximum couch slouch going?

Normally, I recommend adding a bowl of chips or Hostess Donettes for ballast, but optimal spine alignment can be achieved simply through force generated by the sense of existential doom and plenty of loud, heavy sighs.

For that extra despondency through the shoulders, just think about the vacation you have to cancel, plus the possibility of impending food shortages. If that doesn't do it, call me for more suggestions.

April 16, 2020

Fortune Teller

"Come in," a woman's voice said from inside the shop.

It was strange that I could hear her, since the door was closed. But I only realized this later.

Compelled by unseen forces, I walked to the door and opened it. It was pitch black inside until my eyes adjusted. When they did, it was still pitch black.

"You want to know your fortune," the voice said.

It sounded plausible. "Sure."

"Drink lots of water. As for the rest—" Here she paused for effect. "As for the rest, be sure to tell plenty of jokes about chickens."

April 17, 2020

Dream States

"I'm the Decider."

His voice was velvet.

"You want me to decide something for ya? Because I could. I'm the Decider. And my Daddy was the Decider before me."

Oh yeah. This was the best dream ever.

In my dream he was naked, creating oil paintings in his bathtub. There were lots of bubbles, so I couldn't see anything. The easel was placed so he wouldn't splash it when he washed his hair.

"I'm the Decider."

I woke up feeling empty. Funny, what you end up missing from your past, based on what you've got in the present.

April 18, 2020

Echo One

I heard a noise coming from the back bedroom. It wasn't a noise I should hear coming from inside my house, except when watching *The Expanse*. I'm not kidding—it sounded like a tiny spaceship hurtling down the hallway.

I had to see what it was, so I started creeping down the hall when a tiny object hit my arm. It was a little spaceship, flying toward the kitchen. Then I heard voices.

"Base, this is Echo 1. We hit some turbulence but are back on course for the sink, over."

I guess nothing should surprise me anymore.

April 19, 2020

America's #1

America's #1 Donut!

America's #1 Food Additive!

America's #1 Plastic Cup!

America's #1 Mulch!

America's #1 Thursday Night 7pm Drama Comedy about a Woman Who Likes the Color Orange!

America's #1 Drain Cleaner!

America's #1 PVC Pipe!

America's #1 Toothpaste Preferred by Hipsters Between the Ages of 30 and 45 Who Don't Like Mint Flavor!

America's #1 Yarn for Knitting Scarves to Give as Gifts to People Who Are Allergic to Wool!

America's #1 Source for Gel Pens with Blue Ink!

America's #1 Lawn Fertilizer!

America's #1 Source for Mindless Distraction When You Could Be Outside!

America's #1!

April 20, 2020

Oh Jack

One morning, I went on a walk in the park. I noticed him that very first day; sinewy, tall, rooted. Silent.

I went back the next day; he was there again.

Walking in the park became part of my new daily routine. I began to look forward to seeing him there, and I took comfort knowing he would watch over me while I moved across the earth, smelling the morning dew evaporating from the robin-covered grass.

One morning I felt so lonely, I stopped and gave him a hug. "Oh Jack," I sighed.

The tree hugged me back.

April 21, 2020

Tyranny Bagels

Introducing Tyranny Bagels, the most recent venture from Shitstorm Enterprises.

Founded in March 2020, Tyranny Bagels overtly serves most of the Western Hemisphere, with covert operations in over forty countries worldwide (and possibly beyond that, but we'll never tell)!

Our bagels are made expressly for profit. Because our ingredients are secretly sourced from countries we publicly blame for all our problems, Tyranny bagels have that rich, tangy flavor of smug satisfaction while still being heart-friendly and cheap as dirt.

If you're hankering for something filling yet completely full of hot air, try a Tyranny Bagel!

(Calorie count classified.)

April 22, 2020

The Authority

I dreamt I was back in high school. Only I wasn't there as high school me; I was there as now me.

I was in detention. The Authority walked into the room and loomed over me. Faceless, dark.

"You are nothing," The Authority said. "You've made no mark on the world. You might as well not be here at all. If you had never existed, it would not make any difference."

I thought about that. The birds would still sing, the sun would still rise. Just no me.

I said to The Authority, "I am okay with that."

April 23, 2020

Aw Nuts

Norman liked nuts. All kinds of nuts—he wasn't too discerning. He was a squirrel, after all.

One morning, Norman woke up feeling a bit peckish. So, he went off to look for nuts. For breakfast. As he was searching, he ran into his good friend, Edgar.

"I'm looking for nuts," Norman announced.

"I'm looking for bugs!" said Edgar, with a lot of enthusiasm.

They continued to look for breakfast together.

Presently, they were joined by a rather distant acquaintance, Moira.

"I'm looking for breakfast!" proclaimed Moira right before she swooped down and ate Norman.

"Nuts," said Edgar.

April 24, 2020

Please Bloom

I planted a seed in rich, living soil, in a paper pot on my windowsill. I made sure there was warmth and water, and I protected the seed from springtime hail and last-minute frosts.

One day, a sprout popped out of the soil. It happened overnight; I was surprised. The sprout had a little hat—the casing of the seed.

I watered the sprout and watched as it transformed from gangly infant to adventurous youth. Eventually, I took the sprout outside and planted it in the earth.

Now I watch out my window, fingers crossed and heart full.

April 25, 2020

Day 42

It was a beautiful sunny day, so I took my afternoon cappuccino outside and sat in the shade. After a few minutes, Crow came back to visit.

"How've you been?" he asked, eyeing my coffee.

"Not so good," I answered. I didn't want to be negative, but I felt that the truth was in order.

"Oh yeah? How so?" Crow hopped from the fence to the flowerpot next to my chair. Close up, I could see the details of the fine feathers around his eyes and beak. He was a beautiful creature.

"I'm feeling older than I should."

April 26, 2020

Domestic Goddess

I am doing all of the things.

First, I crocheted a blanket as a gift, then moved on to knit a cardigan for myself, because cardigan. Soon, knitting seemed extremely pedestrian so I started baking sourdough bread again. There were a lot of simple carbs in bread, though. I figured I should balance those out with more vegetables, so I dug one, then two garden beds and planted tomatoes, leeks, beets, carrots, lettuce.

What to do with all the veggies? Next came fermenting, soups, roasting. But that made me feel a little too domestic. What next? Auto repair?

April 27, 2020

Guilt Trip

Moses felt bad. Very, very guilty. He knew he shouldn't be feeling good, so that made him feel bad. In fact, he was kind of happy. He felt even worse about that.

What was the point, he wondered, of feeling good, if he wasn't supposed to tell anyone about it? How could he justify happiness when it was more acceptable to complain about everything?

The world was a dumpster fire. Everything sucked and everyone in power was an asshat. But deep in his heart, a tiny spark of joy resided. It was enough to know it was there.

April 28, 2020

GenX Birthday

I'm defined by when I was born. I grew up one of those latchkey kids, at home fending for myself. Left to find my own snacks, watch what I wanted on TV. Left figuring things out for myself.

A little later, I felt it in a different way. An underlying sense of frustration and anger at something that could never be defined. Everything and nothing. Punk rock summed it up. We were mad; we trusted no one; tough shit.

But now, I am older. Have I softened? Maybe. I still feel all those things. Only...I am also satisfied.

April 29, 2020

Flighty Girl

One afternoon, Bernice decided to take a walk.

"Be careful," her mom said, "it's windy out there today. You know how you are."

"Yes, mom."

Bernice's mom was always trying to make sure her daughter didn't blow away. Bernice's mom always told her she was flighty, prone to being an airhead, unable to focus.

Bernice was tired of hearing it.

So she decided to practice grounding.

On her walk that windy day, she sat down to rest and relaxed her shoulders. She imagined her feet rooting in the soil. She sighed, exhaled deeply, and turned into a tree.

April 30, 2020

So Cal

Stan raced down Pacific Coast Highway in his convertible Porsche. He pulled his hat down on his head to make sure his toupee didn't fly off and land in someone else's convertible Porsche.

"So, like, stop at the Starbucks," said his date.

"Sure, babe."

Stan cut across three lanes of traffic and pulled off in Corona Del Mar. There were so many other great things to see here besides a goddamn Starbucks. The secluded tide pools, with hermit crabs and sea anemones. And a way better coffee shop just down the road. But she was built...so she won.

May 1, 2020

Peace Banana

Ook commanded attention wherever he went. He was, after all, king of the jungle. He was a tiny primate who screeched softly but carried a big banana.

The story went like this: Many years ago, Ook came across a magical banana plant. Each piece of miraculous fruit was over two feet long and gave the owner immortality and two wishes. From that day forward, Ook never went anywhere without his magic banana. He was a diehard pacifist and wished for happiness and unlimited bananas for all. Everyone loved living without war, but got really tired of eating bananas.

May 2, 2020

Jimmy's Car

One morning, Jimmy woke up and decided he wanted to buy a car. Which wouldn't be all that remarkable except that Jimmy was a snail.

Jimmy was tired of being late for everything. He needed to go faster.

He went to the car dealership, and after careful deliberation spanning several hours, found one he liked. "I'll take it," he told the salesperson, "if you paint a big letter 'S' on the side."

The salesperson agreed—anything for a sale!

When it was ready, Jimmy sped off in his car. The salesperson remarked, "Look at that 'S' car go!"

May 3, 2020

Poor Suckers

Aw, surfers can't get to the beach.

Oh no, we can't get to the gun shop or the bar, either.

Let's complain!

Our civil liberties are being infringed upon!

Never mind that I might pass a possibly deadly virus to your mother or father, sister or brother or child. Never mind. I have the right to cough anywhere.

I will stand behind the flag and the president and a mask (but only so you can't see who I am), and I will fight you for the right to be unthinking, unfeeling, and a sad example of a human.

May 4, 2020

Egg Whisperer

Freya was known as the Egg Whisperer. The things she could do with eggs—it boggled the mind of ordinary breakfasters.

Poached to perfection. Fried however you liked them. Sunny side up? Soft boiled? Sure. In her sleep, she could cook eggs.

Freya's scrambled eggs were so fluffy, it was practically incomprehensible.

Fortunately, she was also good at frying bacon (real or vegan), and made decent coffee, too. People came from miles around to eat Freya's breakfasts.

But she had a dark secret: her expertise stopped with eggs. She ate nothing but frozen pizzas for lunch and dinner.

May 5, 2020

The Buildup

It makes me laugh when people say, "Oh, you're so relaxed, I love your calm presence."

I smirk and think to myself, "Really!"

Because inside, I feel like I have a huge, heavy core of magma, with toxic gases swirling and sweeping, the pressure building to the point of extreme discomfort until one day I will simply EXPLODE and go back to wherever it is I came from.

Do you ever feel that way? Oh, it's just me?

Maybe it's the refried beans.

Regardless, I take one breath in, and on the exhale, remember to trust infinite intelligence.

May 6, 2020

Back Pain

"It sucks getting old," said Bert. He sat on the edge of the couch, trying to put his socks on. He'd managed to get one almost all the way onto his left foot, but when he tried putting his shoe on, he couldn't because the elastic that was supposed to go around his calf was bunched up on his heel. After another brief struggle he gave up, pulled the sock off, and leaned back.

"Myrna, bring me a beer," said Bert.

Myrna glowered. "That's 'Mom' to you, and you're only ten, so stop it with the beer thing."

May 7, 2020

Computer Glitch

Francis had a really bad case of writer's block, for which there seemed to be no cure. After weeks of trying to trick his brain into thinking he had a story, he gave up and googled "how to overcome writer's block." He started working through the suggestions in the order of popularity (because of course the Goracle knows what's best).

The thirty-eighth suggestion he tried was to rub mayonnaise on his neck. As he sat at his computer with sandwich condiment dripping onto his pants, he realized he'd done the thirty-eighth most popular remedy for anti-aging DIY facials.

May 8, 2020

Magic Shop

Stella browsed the books and baubles in the strange shop. She'd never been inside before, that she could remember. Was it a new store? She walked this street every day but couldn't remember noticing it before.

There were dozens of different candles, with names like "Perfunctory Essence" and "Cosmology." Shelves lined the walls and held glass containers filled with dried plants. She heard the caw of a crow and looked up to see one perched in the rafters. The scent of curiosity was strong.

"Do you have a potion for presidential elections?" Stella asked the shopkeeper.

"Aisle seven."

May 9, 2020

Polyglot Throwdown

"Isn't it just terrible, this virus thing?" Clarice asked the man as she rung up his groceries. He wasn't wearing a mask, she noted with patient contempt.

"I don't want a viral swing," he said. He didn't stop reading his phone as she swiped each item. *Beep!*

"No," she said. "The virus. The COVID-19 thing. It's terrible."

"Did you just call me a furball?" He looked up in alarm.

Beep!

"Where's your mask?" Clarice tried again.

"Oh yeah, oatmeal face mask, good for hydration." He shrugged.

Oh my god, thought Clarice. We're going to hell in a handbasket.

May 10, 2020

Zoom Butt

"Jodi, get your dog's ass out of my face."

Under normal circumstances, this request would've made Jodi mad. She'd just held her dog up for everyone to see how fluffy he was, and in the resulting mayhem, ended up flashing the dog's posterior to her whole team.

"But Sully just had a bath!" she tried to explain.

"I don't care if your dog just ate the Pope; I don't need to see his butt."

"God, Karen, you're so unreasonable." Jodi looked at everyone, but they were all busy writing on nonexistent notepads. She put Sully down and sighed.

May 11, 2020

Sully's Revenge

Sully made sure the hooman called Karen was on the flat screen picture thingie before sneaking out and licking the thin shiny talk object his food giver always pointed at him. Three schnarfles left to right made the territorial alert ring sound.

"Be right back, someone's at the door." The lady sleep pillow waved at the flat screen picture thingie and left the room. The man sleep pillow was gone, presumably to get meat.

It was Sully's big chance.

He jumped up on the empty chair, smiled at Karen, and gave her a show she wouldn't soon forget.

May 12, 2020

Extreme Knitting

I'll knit a scarf while I'm self- isolating, I thought.

That's how it started.

After I'd used all the yarn in my stash and the scarf was forty feet long, I decided to try another angle.

I did some research.

Sent a few emails.

Made some calls.

I met a guy in Durant where I bought a sheep. I quarantined said sheep.

I learned to take care of the sheep, watched it wander my back yard, and hid it from the neighbors (losing battle).

Then I sheared it, combed the fleece, spun some yarn, and started another scarf.

May 13, 2020

Road Trip

Durga spotted Shiva washing his SUV in his driveway again. She moseyed outside for a chat.

"Dude, I'm bored," she complained. "Let's take that thing somewhere." She nodded her chin at Shiva's vehicle.

"Okay," said Shiva. "Where do you want to go?"

"I haven't had ice cream in ages."

Shiva finished drying the last of the water beads off the hood. "Let's roll."

Durga watched Shiva's profile as they drove to Braum's. He was handsome, she reflected. His temples were turning silver. Could this mean the end of another cycle of life and death? Only time would tell.

May 14, 2020

Crow Pose

I hurt my back. Movement was a continual source of pain and disappointment, and the weather echoed my sentiments. During a brief reprieve from thunderstorms and flash flooding, I went outside to watch the cedar waxwings attack the mulberry tree. I had to sit leaning forward and to the left to find a break from my misery.

"You look strange," said Crow, who had seen me sit down and decided to pay a visit.

"I hurt my back," I explained. "What do you do when your back hurts?"

Crow cocked his head and thought about his answer. "Starve."

May 15, 2020

Roll 'Em

"I'm going to make a film," announced Deborah.

Her audience of one, Bob, smiled appreciatively but remained silent.

"Yes," she said. She steepled her fingers as she paced. "I can see it clearly. A short piece, depicting human struggles in a realistic yet uplifting way, during these trying times."

Bob's silence indicated his approval.

"It'll be a story of how we can overcome and adapt to anything that comes our way," Deborah explained, gesticulating wildly as she stopped pacing. "No dialogue, just music."

Bob nodded.

"It'll be the best commercial Rotund Tires has ever made!"

Bob barked loudly.

May 16, 2020

Remember Remembering

Remember sitting around remembering?

When we stole coffee carafes from the fourth floor of the Disneyland Hotel? Driving around in your parents' Studebaker, thinking we was smart...

Remember going off to college? You aimed high; I shot so low I'd be sure to hit the mark. That time we went to Peyton Reed's house and thought we were all grown up.

Remember not seeing each other for years and years? You had kids; I had multiple identity crises.

Careers, vacations, pets, husbands, food, heartache. Picking up each time we see each other, like we're still in high school.

May 17, 2020

Some Times

Sometimes we grieve for things that are no more. Will they return? If so, when?

With time, we find a new normal. Things won't seem scary or sad someday. But does that mean it's not okay to feel that way now?

The other night I dreamt about my mother. She was in her bedroom sleeping; I was in mine. A storm came through. The house shook with thunder and wind; impending doom was right outside the windows. I ran to warn her, but she kept sleeping. The dream ended suddenly, and I realized you cannot wake the dead.

May 18, 2020

Grandma Neil

Grandma Neil lived by the ocean. She'd go out her front door and sink her toes into the hot summer sand of Sunset Beach.

Grandma Neil was married once, but I suspect being a single gal suited her much better. She went ballroom dancing, visited friends, and had oodles of "pen pals."

Grandma Neil drove a white Buick and drank instant coffee after her afternoon nap. She wore a sunhat and took me for walks on the beach to collect shells. She wrote down the stories I told her, before I could read. Grandma Neil was a badass.

May 19, 2020

Cryptid Quarantine

Squatchie didn't understand what the big deal was. Why were people so afraid to be by themselves? He'd been self-isolating for years. And he was a perfectly adjusted, happy monster.

One Wednesday morning, Squatchie was washing the dishes after making some breakfast (quail eggs and acorn mush, he wasn't a philistine) when he heard an unusual noise. He put his Calphalon pan down and slowly turned around. A bush shook violently, and all the hair on his neck, hands, arms, legs, and feet stood on end.

"There you are!" said Mrs. Squatchie.

Damn. His 20-year quarantine was over.

May 20, 2020

Weed Pulling

It was a beautiful morning. I'd just watered my veggie garden and stood looking at all the weeds.

"And, like, I just don't feel like he's growing as a person."

"I know, like, totally."

The voices approached the yard: two women out for a walk.

"His, like, brothers? They are like, growing as people but there are like, traits, you know? That are totally still there."

"Unh."

"And like, you know? I feel like, it is not fair to me because I am like, doing all this growth and stuff."

I suddenly felt compelled to pull the weeds.

May 21, 2020

Crow Flies

Crow visited this afternoon as I sat in the garden with my cappuccino.

"You're looking well," I said, eyeing his shiny feathers as he settled his wings.

He puffed up his chest. "Thank you. Why wouldn't I?"

"I read yesterday this country has lost 30% of its bird population in the last fifty years."

"What's a country?" Crow asked. "And for that matter, what's a year?"

I sighed. It was easy to take on the guilt of the entire human race when talking to a crow.

"Anyway," he added, "none of that prevents me from loving to fly."

May 22, 2020

The Purge

Last night I dreamt my cell phone threw up.

Photos from Belize, 2013.

The value of my retirement accounts.

A record of all the books I've read since it became necessary to document them on a server so no one could give a shit (which, by my expert calculation, was the summer of 2014).

PTSD-induced rantings from 2012 in a password-protected journaling app.

All 1,880 photos I've posted on Instagram since 2011 (Insta OldSkool).

Words with Fucking Friends.

Music, memories, remembering, pictures, politics, recipes, passwords—my phone hurled it all, making a huge mess on the kitchen counter.

May 23, 2020

Street Cred

Earl watched his son, Earl Junior, with parental disdain. The kid was sitting on the couch with his earbuds in, singing along to some rap song. Lyrics about bitches and dope and fornication and whatnot. It made no sense in the suburbs.

Earl threw a pillow at Junior, who angrily pulled an earbud out. "What?"

"Go walk the dog," said Earl.

Junior put his earbud back in and continued to sing about dope.

Earl took off his shoe and threw it at Junior.

Finally Junior stomped off to walk the poodle. *Damn kids,* thought Earl. *Don't know jack.*

May 24, 2020

Modern Woman

What would Miss Fisher do if she were living in the Age of Coronavirus? She was all that and a vodka martini, a hundred years ago. If she were here, she would find ways to thrive.

She'd solve crimes while lounging by her pool, looking fabulous. A six-course meal would be served daily at seven. She'd seduce DI Robinson into having phone sex. He'd be embarrassed at first, but then secretly look forward to it all day till he could get home and call her—ostensibly to catch up on an investigation. Miss Fisher would do it all.

May 25, 2020

Life Questions

Am I a germophobe, or am I just being cautious?

Am I a compassionate human, or am I "on the spectrum" and not sure how to understand the subtleties of human behavior?

Am I afraid to grow old, or do I never want to grow up?

How do I tell if I'm doing this right?

What if there is no "right?"

What if all that matters is that I'm kind and caring to the planet I live on, to the others who inhabit it, and most of all, to myself?

What if I am actually doing it right?

May 26, 2020

See Monster

Gilly lived in the middle of the U.S. Which was great for some reasons, all of which had escaped her since mid-March. She was landlocked and bummed.

One day Gilly loaded up her dishwasher and turned it on. It started making horrible noises that sounded like roaring. She turned it off and opened it. Inside was a monster.

"Excuse me, but do you know the way to the deep sea?" it asked.

"There's a monster in my dishwasher," was all she said.

"Apparently your dishwasher is a magical portal to the ocean," said the monster.

"Sweet. Let's go."

May 27, 2020

Super Power

There is a girl I know who has an uncanny ability to find things. It's a superpower of sorts.

People hire her to help them find things. Sometimes, they tell the girl what they've lost, and she looks for it and then finds it. Other times, a person knows they've lost something, but they don't know what. It's just a feeling they have—that something is missing. So they ask her to figure out what they've lost, and then find it.

She herself is lost and can never be found. It's why she's so good at finding things.

May 28, 2020

Hundred Thousand

A break from the rain found me outside drinking my afternoon cappuccino. I was deep in thought, pondering the state of things, and didn't hear Crow land on the fence.

"You look...I don't know what the word is," he said, making me jump a little.

"Sad," I supplied.

"But it's such a nice day."

"A lot of people have died, though, from this virus thing. Everyone's mad at each other and..." I gave up.

"It's the natural order of things," explained Crow.

I laughed at that. "Is not. It's all man-made ridiculousness."

"And it's still the natural order."

May 29, 2020

Bee Love

Evie loved flowers. At the end of one particularly hard winter, she bought as many packets of wildflower seeds as she could afford. Hundreds of them. She read the back of each package to determine when they should be sown, and when it was time, she tossed seeds everywhere. Front yard, back yard, everywhere.

When the flowers bloomed, bees from miles around came to visit. They loved her house, and they loved her. One day she walked outside and was surrounded by bees. They gently picked her up, professed their love, and took her back to their hive.

May 30, 2020

Yoga Bandit

You want a private lesson but don't want anyone to know? Feeling a little funky in your down dog, and you're not sure if you should really be feeling *that* funky? Do you find yourself wondering "am I doing this right" at least four times during your Zoom yoga practice?

Well, never fear! The Yoga Bandit has got you covered. For a nominal fee (plus an astronomical surcharge), the Yoga Bandit will make their way into your back yard and provide you with personalized, (almost) hands-on instruction.

Feel great in Warrior I! Nail your Side Angle Pose! Namaste!

May 31, 2020

Goddess Reprise

The carrots are growing tall, and today for lunch we ate salads.
Bowls piled high with lettuce freshly picked from our garden,
and not much else because tomorrow is store
day.
One haircut has occurred,
turning my partner from Beethoven
on a calorie-restricted diet
to Miller from *The Expanse*.
A suitable exchange, if you ask me.
I made three cappuccinos today, one for a porch-perching guest, one for me, and one for my man.
Laundry is done.
The windows are open, letting in the warm breeze because soon
it will be too hot to breathe the summer air.

June 1, 2020

Earth Visit

During mediation, I called on my mother.

"Mom?"

Silence.

"Mom?"

"Oh! Sorry, I was catching up on all the *Muppet Show* episodes."

I smiled. "Those are good memories."

"I know, right? Wacka-wacka!"

"Mom?"

"Yes?"

"How am I doing?"

She sighed. "Andrea. You are amazing. An amazing woman. All of consciousness loves you—loves all of you. All of the women who came before you stand with you. When you tell a story, we smile. When you write a book, we cheer. When you laugh, we dance. It is that way for all humankind, for all eternity."

Don't forget.

June 2, 2020

Wrong Move

Beads of sweat popped out all over Wanda's forehead. One inappropriate move and it would all be over.

Should she take a step to the left? It looked safe, but it could be quicksand over there. What about to the right? The water didn't appear deep; she thought she could see the bottom just a few inches under the surface. But as she well knew, that water could be much deeper than it looked.

She'd gotten this far by moving carefully and slowly. But she was in the middle of it now, and couldn't afford a wrong move.

June 3, 2020

The Pro

"Thanks for getting that guy killed for me. He was one bad dude!"

"Sure."

"And they disposed of the body! I don't see a trace. Except for that wet carpet over there. But I opened the windows and everything's fine!"

"Unh. You want to go with us into space?"

"Do I ever!"

Kitchen detaches from house; countertop turns into ship controls. They fly around space and come back.

"That was awesome! Hey, can I give you some money, for my share?"

"Really. You want to give me money for your share of flying my kitchen around in space?"

June 4, 2020

Where Cut

"I want to get my hair cut," said Peggy. "But where should I go?"

Options were limited. The part of the country she lived in was under martial law. The West Coast had broken off and fallen into the ocean the previous week. It had finally been overcome by the stress fractures associated with chronic indignation. The East Coast had built themselves a wall, and to get over it at any of the three access points (New York, Florida or Washington, DC) required a down payment of $4mil.

So Peggy made an appointment with Musk's stylist, on Mars.

June 5, 2020

Keep Digging

"Tell us a story, Grampy!"

"Hmmm. Lemme see now. Well, there was the time I decided to construct me one of them swimming pool things. I got me a shovel, started digging, and pretty soon I started hearing this awful noise. Then I hit a crevice and steamy, vile-smelling gas started pouring out!"

"Oh no! Then what Grampy?"

"Then I kept on digging, of course. And pretty soon, that noise turned into 70s rock and I fell right through into the devil's living room."

"Then what?"

"Well then we had dinner. Worst chili dogs I ever did eat."

June 6, 2020

Getting Crafty

"Send in the choppers, we need an extraction."

Gerald was confused. "I'm sorry, what?"

"We've got a situation. Send backup to rendezvous point Sierra Hotel India Tango. Repeat. Shitstorm One."

"Okay, but..." Gerald got out his pencil. "Could you, uh, say that again, please?"

"Negative! Negative! Operation Shitstorm!"

Gerald started to sweat. What did all this mean? Sierra what? The voice sounded serious. He scribbled some indecipherable notes: *Shitstorm.*

"Do you copy?"

"I'm trying to copy, but you're talking too fast," said Gerald. "Say, who is this?"

Pause.

"Who is *this*?" the voice asked.

"Gerald. At JoAnn's Fabrics?"

June 7, 2020

Bigfoot Complex

Some days, Squatchie just couldn't even. Like, it was all just one big hassle. Why even get up and out of the cave in the morning? It was hard being mysterious all the time.

As soon as he'd woken, he knew it was going to be one of those days. He sighed plaintively and meandered outside to see about breakfast. It was already hot and dammit but he just felt like moping. He gnawed on a root and felt sorry for himself.

Some days he just wanted a cuddle and a quiet float in the pool, you know?

June 8, 2020

Jungle Cat

They say nature takes back the streets. Vegetation grows wild. Creatures lurk around every corner. Like me, the ferocious jungle cat.

I prowl, making myself seen when I want to, invisible when needed. I track my prey and kill to eat.

Today I patrol the edge of my domain. It's dangerous here; my enemies wish me gone and show no mercy. But today I will leave my mark. I will enter the yard of the lady who despises me because I eat the birds she feeds. I will poop in the pot where she grows her dill plants.

June 9, 2020

Selective Rememberin'

Damon had selective memorying. Or was it selectorative memorizing? He'd written it down on a scrap of paper so he could remember, but then he forgot where he put it.

He could remember the last episode of that show with the two crazy guys, when they were mad at each other and everyone voted on which guy they liked best. But he couldn't remember the name of the show, or who the guys were.

Damon remembered that other show, where everyone was mad at each other and the world was a mess…but he couldn't remember how it ended.

June 10, 2020

Two Sides

Inside

Hello, lowly sparrow. You're so plain. Grey, brown, black, white. Your incessant single chirp, over and over—the ubiquitous sound of a small mind. You make your way through the neighborhood in gangs of simple-minded cohorts, looking for free food and annoying places to nest.

Outside

Hello, lowly human. Sitting in your gigantic box—why do you need such a big box? You sit in there, paying imaginary birdseed to pretend to control your environment. Temperature, brightness, noise level. You occasionally get into small metal boxes, moving around at high speeds to feel important, pretending to care.

June 11, 2020

Love Love

Love love love love sunsets love love love laughter love love coffee ice cream love love love knitting love love music love sex love love love ocean love sunshine love love love love birds love flowers love love reading love love cookies love love inspiration love love writing love chickens love romance love love love love family love love friends love love love joy love freedom love love loving kindness love words love love love strong hands love love love peace love humans love love love love all beings love love love universe love love love love you.

June 12, 2020

The Formation

"It's no use. We can't fight him alone." Shiva shifted uncomfortably in his chair.

Vishnu looked at Shiva, then to Brahma. They were sitting around a folding table in Shiva's garage and the harsh fluorescent bulb was not a kind light. "It's true. It's unsustainable."

Brahma sighed. "We must create something more powerful. A new ally, perhaps."

Shiva looked past Brahma and Vishnu to the ring of cohorts sitting beyond their power triangle. They nodded their agreement. "Make the call," he said.

Brahma pulled out his phone and dialed. They heard the ring right outside the garage door.

June 13, 2020

Same Game

Miss Fisher is faring well in the age of coronavirus. To paraphrase an idiom that she would never be caught dead using, the rules had changed but the game is still the same. Can she meet DI Robinson for a cocktail at her favorite downtown hotel? Yes, but she won't. It is not safe, and her life is worth more than her need to be seen.

Miss Fisher still solves mysteries via her poolside chaise and has learned to make do with ordering takeout. And of course she still calls her favorite lover, Jack, every night before bed.

June 14, 2020

Lost Girl

"I heard you know how to find things."

I leaned on the frame of the open car window and looked at him. He had mischievous eyes peering up at me from under brown curls, but I could tell he was legit. "Maybe," I said. Experience had taught me, never commit too early to a job.

He shifted to one side, and my muscles tensed as he reached in the back pocket of his jeans. He pulled out a crumpled business card and handed it to me.

It was my card.

I never have to go looking for work.

June 15, 2020

Stupid Fence

One Woof Charlie paced the backyard, frustrated at the lack of vision. Yes of course, his owners were incredibly shortsighted, but that wasn't the lack of vision he was thinking of just now. Rather, he was lamenting that the infernal humans had removed the chain link fence—through which he could view the comings and goings along the street—and replaced it with a tall cedar fence. Now he couldn't see shit.

He stopped suddenly and cocked his head, raising one ear. Was that a rabbit? Or a car door? Or maybe a pork chop? He barked once.

June 16, 2020

Backward Forward

"Dammit, Jim, it won't turn!" Diane moved the key in the ignition switch as far as it would go each direction. ON-OFF-ON-OFF-ON-OFF.

"Careful, Diane, we just got the garage fixed from the last time you had trouble."

It was just like Jim to bring up the past. And not in a good way, either. Where was the man she married? The man who skinny-dipped in the community pool at midnight, and wanted to make out in the grocery store? Now it was all, "Don't destroy the garage again, Diane."

She turned it to ON and floored it. Again.

June 17, 2020

The Visit

Durga felt refreshed and rejuvenated as she took her walk. Ever since she had been recreated by Shiva and the gang, she'd felt like a new entity. It was…liberating.

Her wandering took her to the neighborhood park. She stood watching a turtle, who was watching a man dig the earth, destroying what used to be the turtle's home.

"Makes you wonder," said a voice.

Durga turned to see Crow, perched on a stop sign.

"Yes." She sighed thoughtfully. Durga stood tall, putting her hands on her hips. "Come on," she said to Crow. "We've got work to do."

June 18, 2020

Toasted Coconut

"Bert!" snapped Myrna as she read her ladies' magazine. "Stop procrastinating and make those cookies."

Bert was slouching on the couch. He sighed heavily at his mom's command. It was so unfair that kids had to do what their parents said.

He went to the kitchen and looked through the Walmart bag on the table. He'd even had to go into the store and shop for the ingredients.

An hour later, Myrna wandered into the kitchen. "What's the holdup? And the weird smell?"

"The coconut won't toast," said Bert, pointing to the hairy orb in the toaster oven.

June 19, 2020

Doctor Recommended

Doctor JJ back with you, checking in live from Tulsa, Oklahoma, with a few more self-isolation, protesting, super-spreader Juneteenth health tips!

Now I'm sure you're all aware it's a good idea to build muscle strength as well as endurance and cardio fitness! You never know when you might need to outrun zombies with offensive flags, airborne germs, or the National Guard. You may also need to hold your breath for hours at a time, so be prepared!

My expert advice: write your mayor a love letter, break out the snacks, and pray like you've never prayed before. Onward!

June 20, 2020

The Introduction

Durga put her plate in the dishwasher and checked the clock. "Crow," she called through the open window, "let's go."

She made her way outside, and Crow landed on her left shoulder as she walked toward Shiva's house a few doors down. She let herself in the side door of his garage, which had been converted into one of those stupid mancaves. Durga couldn't understand the appeal.

"Hiya fellas," she said, pulling up a chair.

"Welcome," said Shiva. Vishnu nodded.

"Thanks."

Crow was silent out of respect, but hopped nervously from foot to foot.

It was almost time.

June 21, 2020

Higher Ed

"I'm now officially done with school," said Wanda. "So, like, you can suckit."

"Oh yeah?" her mom asked. "Okay! What's next?"

"Well, it just so happens I had a job interview last week, and I got an offer."

"Great! Is it related to your major?"

Wanda hesitated. "Uh huh," she half-heartedly replied.

"You got all A's, right?"

"One B."

"Suma cum laude, and Phi Beta Kappa?"

Wanda wondered where her mother was going with this. "So?"

"So, what's next?"

"As soon as I get back from touring with the Dead for three weeks, I start at B Dalton."

June 22, 2020

Camo Frog

"Alvin!"

Silence.

"Al?" Dotty's stomach dropped. "Al! You show yourself this instant!"

Al was always doing stuff like this, fretted Dotty. Making her think something bad happened, when the whole time he was hiding right in front of her. Just because he blended in with the plants didn't give him the right.

"Show yourself or I swear, I'll really leave you this time!"

"Brrrrrrrrrrrit!" Alvin hopped from the frog-shaped flowerpot and landed on the sidewalk right in front of Dotty. "You didn't see me, did—"

Moira the hawk swooped down and had herself a little froggy snack.

June 23, 2020

Tough Chicks

"Don't talk to me about personal responsibility," griped Iris as she scratched the dry ground. It hadn't rained in weeks and everyone was a little on edge. "You don't know what it's like out here. I swear, Beryl, you changed when you ran off with Bigfoot. It's like I don't even know you anymore."

Beryl watched her friend and thought about her words. It was probably true. Squatchie had shown her another life out there in the wilderness, a life far different from the hen house. "What can I say?" said Beryl. "A chicken's got to be free."

June 24, 2020

New Math

NO CALCULATOR NEEDED

distance = 6 feet

velocity = sneeze + cough – mask

mask effectiveness = ability to sew + fabric – amazon – testosterone

survival possibility = (new cases + political party) * IQ

aptitude rate = +(introvert)^2 * -(extrovert) / streaming services + books

if streaming services = 0, then AR = AR * IQ

if human IQ < cheeto IQ, then (you're screwed)

survival rate = (love + compassion – hate) * (2020 – 2020) + 2021

hope + love + laughter = friends

friend + friend = connection

connection – social media > facebook

Me + You = Happy.

June 25, 2020

Repeat Repeat

How long ago was before? Before what? Was that normal? Or is now normal? If this is normal, what is it? When is the future? If the future isn't here yet, what are we in now? Or what were we next month? What will we be last week?

I feel different this week than I did last week. But maybe it's the same as the week before. Everything was different two weeks ago. But that's normal, and also the same. Things are now, and will be next week. We've all been here before, so let's just eat chocolate.

June 26, 2020

Getting Rest

"Remember when we were kids," said Shiva, "and we would play war in the ravine behind the neighborhood?" He leaned back in his patio chair and sipped his tea.

Durga laughed. "I remember. I would always win."

"You always cheated!"

"Maybe," she said cryptically. "But maybe not."

"Spoken like a true politician."

"I'm not a politician. I'm a warrior who can kick your ass, even now."

Shiva held up his palm. "Not necessary. You know we will always be great friends."

They watched the sun set behind the maple tree as Crow settled in the branches to sleep.

June 27, 2020

Hold Fast

It had been a tough week. On Saturday, Cherise decided to go for a walk in the park. She made her way past some benches, where another woman sat alone, reading a book. Suddenly there was a heavy *thump* noise. The woman on the bench looked up to discover Cherise's right arm had fallen off.

"Oh dear," Cherise said. "That's never happened before."

Then Cherise's other arm fell off. They both stared at it—motionless on the gravel path.

"Hmmm," said Cherise. "This is most unusual."

Next, both her legs fell off. It had been a tough week.

June 28, 2020

Yuge Problem

"Whaddya mean 'it's not so bad,' Donny? My arms and legs fell off." Cherise looked down at her torso, wondering how she was ever going to get pajamas on that night.

"Everything's fine, Cherise, you look tremendous, just fantastic, I can't even tell you don't got arms, I mean, lookit your beautiful blue eyes. They look YUGE!"

Cherise felt good. It had been years since Don had complimented her. But it didn't change the fact she couldn't drive her car. "But Donny, now you have to take care of me."

Don looked at his watch. "Damn, gotta go!"

June 29, 2020

Deep Water

Ellory "Ellie" McFinn dipped her big toe into the pool.

"Perfect," she said. As she let her thin cotton robe flutter to the ground, revealing her slender frame clad only in a sleek, black one-piece swimsuit, Detective Robinson began to feel light-headed.

"Miss McFinn, if you please, can we keep to the subject at hand?"

"Which was what, exactly, Jack?" Ellie glided into the water, not stopping until she was in up to her neck. "I seem to be in up to my neck," she added, with a smile playing on her red lips.

"Me too," mumbled Jack.

June 30, 2020

Good Times

"You okay?" I asked.

"Yes. Yup. Good. Fine."

I didn't believe her, but the last thing I wanted to do was say I didn't believe her.

"Feeling all right?" I tried again.

"Uh huh, good. Feeling great. Excellent."

"You look a little…" How should I finish that sentence?

"A little what? How do I look? Do I look like something's wrong? Because nothing's wrong. Everything is perfect. Really really good."

"I'm just not sure—"

"If you ask me one more time, I'm not going to be fine anymore. One more question will send me over the edge."

July 1, 2020

Good Advice

"Well, you see," said Bigfoot, "in order to remain an enigma, you simply must keep certain things a secret." He smiled coyly. "Only the bare essentials—so to speak—should be revealed. A closed book romance, as it were."

I nodded and knit my brows, indicating I was giving his words serious consideration. After all, it wasn't every day I got advice from Sasquatch.

"That is what you wanted to know, isn't it? How to write a strong male lead?"

I hesitated. "Well, I really just wanted to know how to get back to the highway, but okay."

July 2, 2020

Pasadena Hijinks

I tried to retire at sixty-seven, like a normal senior. I left with a good pension and even found a decent Medicare gap plan. I still had my own teeth, and I got to spend time with my teenage granddaughter. It should have been perfect.

But then they discovered my handler was a double agent. Some drugs went missing, and I got kidnapped and had to bust my way out by shoving a pencil so far up a goon's nose he could write with the top of his head. And now here I am, back in the game.

July 3, 2020

Bitter Sweet

"This doesn't taste good."

"Stop complaining. Just eat it."

Darius again took the strange fruit in both hands and bit into it. This time it tasted different. He saw the flavors, swirling and blending, floating up to the sky. He felt like his feet had left the ground, and in an instant, he could see everything.

"Oh," he said.

"Yes, son," said his mother. "You are connected to every living thing. You know what they know. You see what they do."

Darius began to cry.

"It's all right, child. Just be kind, and you will always be free."

July 4, 2020

Sunny Day

Ellie McFinn stretched out on the chaise by the pool so that Detective Inspector Robinson couldn't help but notice her legs' length and shape. She watched his eyes travel along them and up her torso to her face. She smiled but said nothing.

"Erm," said DI Robinson, who seemed to be incapable of forming complete sentences.

"I believe you had a question for me, Jack." Ellie adjusted her wrap to fall in a more modest arrangement. It did the trick.

The color returned to Jack's face. "Miss McFinn, I've come to ask for your help on a case."

July 5, 2020

The Tiger

"Let's begin, shall we?" Shiva quieted everyone in his mancave; the silence was palpable.

Suddenly, Durga had a vision of when she and Shiva went for ice cream in the spring. So long ago. Such innocence.

"Everyone has brought you gifts," said Vishnu, laying one hundred marigolds on the card table before her.

One by one, the men came forward to give her their offerings. Flowers, weapons, and talismans were placed on the table. A tiger lay at her feet.

"Thank you," she said when they had finished. "But the ultimate cost will be more than these gifts."

July 6, 2020

What Now?

Mad, frustrated, scared, confused. Voiceless. Was that me then, or me now?

I feel sad. Will anything I do make any sort of difference? Should I be concerned by my lack of concern? What if I don't amount to anything? Is there anything I can say to make anything better than it was? What if my inability to think about the future is due to being totally overwhelmed by the present? What am I supposed to be doing right now? How can I ever get it right if all I can see is how to get it wrong?

July 7, 2020

Second Opinion

Doctor Mister with you, filling in for Doctor JJ, who sadly, due to his refusal to "mask up," contracted a rare strain of Stupid Sickness and is currently self-isolating in a cardboard box. But don't worry, I'm here today to give you a few tips on beating that summer heat!

When the day seems like it'll never end, your week just keeps going, and you feel like you'll be stuck in this oven called July till sometime next April, just remember to dip your toes in the water, chant your mantra, and take a nap. And bingo-bongo: nirvana!

July 8, 2020

Movie Deal

"Female lead cavorts on holiday with gal pal. They discover a body, and—"

"Cavorts?"

"Hangs out, bums around, two friends go to the beach. Whatever. They find a body, see, and call the police."

"Is this modern day?"

"What do you mean by 'modern'? Is it futuristic? No. Are they Pilgrims? No. Maybe they're flappers. What's it matter?"

"I need to see it in my mind's eye."

"Okay fine, whatever, it's the 1970s, okay? Short shorts, feathered bangs, that kind of shit."

"The girls are hot?"

"Very. Anyways, they help the police solve the murder."

"I'm in."

July 9, 2020

Big Changes

I read that you can switch up your life by changing your brain patterns. Sounded good! I decided to start with something simple. I began putting my left sock on before my right (usually it was the other way around). I lost five pounds!

Then I started putting on my shorts left leg first. I got a book and movie deal! Started eating dinner for breakfast, and won the lottery. Walking sideways brought me the love of my life. Now I drive everywhere in reverse. Takes longer to go someplace, but I can't wait to see what happens!

95/100

July 10, 2020

The Surface

Freya decided to go kayaking. One Saturday, after a breakfast of particularly fluffy scrambled eggs served with feta and wilted spinach, she went to the kayak store. She bought a one-person kayak and had the shopkeeper help her tie it to the top of her car.

She drove an hour north to a beautiful lake, where she dragged the kayak from the car into the water and pushed off.

It was quiet on the water. Only birds above, fish below. No words or shouts or laughter or crying. Just wind. She paddled to the center of the lake.

July 11, 2020

Good Luck

Durga completed the online form to pause her mail service, then fed Tiger a raw steak. She looked at all the gifts she'd gotten from the guys, which were laid out on the living room floor. Picking out the ones she deemed most useful, she placed some in a backpack and the biggest ones she carried.

Tiger licked his furry jaws and Durga nodded. When they left the house, Crow was waiting in the tree. He cawed anxiously when he saw them.

Night was falling. Shiva stood in his driveway next to his shiny SUV, and waved once.

July 12, 2020

Only Temporary

A thunderstorm came through last night. It began with brilliant flashes of lightning streaking across the evening sky. The wind picked up, and rain spattered the windows. I didn't think much of it. It's summer; we always have storms. They blow through, then it's quiet again.

But last night, the storm became so fierce, I grew frightened. The house shook, creaking and shuddering violently. The power went out. The wind was so loud, it sounded like a freight train coming at us. Then, as if it suddenly remembered it needed to be somewhere else, the storm was gone.

July 13, 2020

The Vanquisher

Thunder rolled across the sky and was as loud as the universe itself. The fury of Durga was unleashed. She raised her sword and in one clean stroke, beheaded the giant demon. His entire army had been defeated.

In the eye of the storm, it was now calm. Crow sat on Durga's shoulder, and when the clouds began to break apart, he left her and flew to the sea, where he found a single white pearl on the sand. He brought it back to her, as she stood with Shiva atop the tallest mountain, looking at the devastation.

July 14, 2020

Swimming Lessons

Squatchie bobbed along the surface of the cool water, looking up at the clouds. How did his heavy body manage to float, even with all that hair? He didn't know, and at that moment he didn't care.

He had tried to order an inflatable pool off Amazonian, but to get one big and deep enough to hold his mighty frame, would have cost an arm and a leg's worth of fur. Instead, he'd taken a risk and headed for the lake.

He sighed heavily and smiled. He was all by himself.

Everything was absolutely perfect in this moment.

July 15, 2020

Beautiful Days

"It's a beautiful day," I said to Crow.

Crow nodded and resettled his wings. "Every day is beautiful."

"Some days are hard."

"The two states aren't mutually exclusive."

I leaned back and looked up at the clouds. I hurt all over, as if something deep in my muscles had been released but was causing pain as it left my body. Perhaps, I thought, when whatever it was had finally been freed, I would feel lightness and freedom.

"I need to rest," I said. "I'm so tired."

Crow landed on my shoulder. "That is what these days are for."

KEEP IN TOUCH

Want free stories, special discounts and ... did I mention free stories?
Sign up for the AceWrites Newsletter - a monthly email full of funness.
Visit acneil.com/flash-free for more info and receive a free short story.

BOOKS BY ANDREA C. NEIL

THE BEVERLEY GREEN ADVENTURES

Beverley Green's First Adventure

Beverley Green's First Territorial Christmas

Beverley Green Finds True North

Beverley Green Comes Home

The Guthrie Short Stories

FLASH FICTION

Days Are Beautiful: 100 flash fiction stories

No Surprises: 100 flash fiction stories

Visit acneil.com/flash-free to stay in the loop and receive a free story!

ACKNOWLEDGMENTS

A heartfelt thanks to my Quarantine Buddies. Hopefully you all know who you are. I couldn't have gotten this far without you. In fact, if it weren't for you, I'd still be curled up in a ball under the bed, eating nothing but single-serving yogurt cups that Marcus slides to me on an Ikea tray.

Thank you to everyone who has read a story, bought a book, taken a yoga class, offered a kind word, sent mail, and laughed at my jokes—or at least pretended to.

And a big ol' *merci* to Bruce Hughes for letting me share the title of this book with the title of one of his songs. "Days are Beautiful" can be found on his *Trap Door* CD that was released in 2013. Bruce, your music has been a source of light during dark times. Thanks.

One day, we will look back at 2020 and laugh heartily, shaking our heads at the supreme weirdness of it all. Till then, let's hold hands over Zoom and eat peanut butter straight out of the jar.

-A

ABOUT THE AUTHOR

Andrea is a writer, editor, and professional introvert. She balances all that with embarrassingly large servings of chocolate, peanut butter straight out of the jar, and plenty of irony. Not to be mistaken for ironing. She doesn't do any of that.

She's a Southern California native, but now calls Tulsa, Oklahoma home, where she lives with her partner and a million houseplants. Favorite pastimes include starting knitting projects, making vegetable soup, and lamenting over the existential qualities of housework.

Andrea is the niece of Eleanor and Francis Coppola, and appreciates all their inspiration and encouragement.

acneil.com

facebook.com/andreacneil

instagram.com/andreacneil

bookbub.com/authors/andrea-c-neil